Victoria Harwood

Three Stories
about
DRAGONS
Book 6

This book from a wonderful collection
"One Hundred Bedtime Stories".
Each story covers a different theme, such as kindness,
friendship, discovery, love, and the diversity of living
creatures in both our world and imaginary ones.
Perfect for young readers.

2

Five Dragon Scales

We occasionally travel around France, and I would notice something unusual on some of the tiles or roof coverings on older houses and churches. These tiles reminded me of dragon scales. I took photographs and examined them closely; there was no doubt - these were either really dragon scales or someone copied them and made tiles based on their design. Can you imagine that there were once people who saw living dragons?

It then that I remembered an interesting story about a dragon. Maybe some fairy whispered it to me? Quite possible!

Long ago, either in the mountains or in mysterious caves by the sea, far from people, dragons lived. Dragons always live alone, it seems. I expect they do not need company if they are already wise and beautiful and everyone fears them.

So, this particular dragon in our story lived in splendid isolation; no one bothered him. Few people knew where it lived. Maybe once every hundred or hundred and fifty years, dragons would meet each other to exchange news and enjoy interacting with their fellow creatures.

Our Dragon had the magnificent name Fiery Wind. He lived in a vast and dark cave in the mountains. Maybe not very high up compared with other dragons.

In front of the cave were slightly hilly plains, forests, rivers, and flat meadows with grass and wildflowers. Our dragon liked everything, and this life suited him. Occasionally, he would leave the cave to fly or soar with the winds among the mountains and hills. Fiery Wind loved to fly through the clouds. Its scales would get covered with millions of drops of water. This made it feel good.

Do you know that clouds only consist of many water droplets?

Fiery Wind also liked to rise above the clouds, where the view was breathtaking. If you think that dragons are bloodthirsty and need food, then you are mistaken.

Dragons are mythical creatures from a completely different reality. They receive energy and strength from the sun, wind, air, and earth. I don't know how they do it, and that's not what this story is about.

Near where Fiery Wind lived, there were many different animals and birds. Eagles, hawks, foxes, marmots, hares, rabbits, deer, goats, wild boars, wolves, monitor lizards, nimble weasels and more. They lived their simple life, raised their offspring, and were either friends with each other or kept their distance, but all this fuss did not interest our dragon; he was above this ordinary life.

Fiery Wind was larger than other dragons; who would want to be friends with him? Even birds did not fly into his cave; only a family of bats considered this place safe, flying out in a swarm at dusk to hunt.

So, days and years passed. One day, Fiery Wind heard through a dream that someone was sitting on his head and moving from side to side. No, it was not something heavy; on the contrary, it was light and fluffy. He opened his eyes and tried to figure out who it was. But he didn't see anything. The Fiery Wind looked up. A small fluffy tail fell into his view. This was already too much! The dragon slowly stood up on all four legs and shook its head from side to side.

But the stranger did not fall to the ground, as one might expect, but instead settled more comfortably between two horns.

Fiery Wind was a little taken aback and even confused by such impudence, not knowing what to do. He was not really a kind dragon, more of a condescending one. Since the creature on his head did not cause him too much trouble, the dragon decided to wait until it had fully woken up, so he laid down again and waited.

He fell asleep again and was later awakened by a strange whistling sound. Do you know how marmots whistle in the mountains? The unexpected whistle was no longer heard from above his head but from behind.

The dragon looked around and saw a fat marmot waddling along its tail, touching its scales and whistling as he did so.

Surprising himself, Fiery Wind did not want to scare the silly little marmot but carefully watched him. The marmot, waddling from paw to paw, touching the thorny protrusions, slowly approached the sharp tip of the dragon's tail. He felt the gaze of Fiery Wind, turned around sharply, and, in surprise, fell on his back, comically raising his hind legs in the air. This sight made Fiery Wind laugh out loud.

You can't even imagine how loud dragons laugh. It was so loud it seemed like a rockfall in the mountains.

laugh. It was so loud it seemed like a rockfall in the mountains. But doing so gave the Dragon great pleasure since he had not laughed so much for a few hundred years.

Fiery Wind was so huge, and the marmot was so small that it all seemed quite absurd.

"Now tell me what brought you to my cave?" the dragon said as quietly as possible, carefully examining the marmot. He had never paid attention to these little whistling, plump creatures before, although he knew they lived around.

"Fairy tales," the marmot stammered.

"What fairy tales?" Fiery Wind frowned slightly.

"Everyone knows about dragons only from fairy tales and legends, but for some reason, no one has seen them. So, I decided to go and find one for myself. My grandfather told me that in ancient times, dragons lived in large caves..."

"And you left your family and your home to find me?" the dragon tilted its head in surprise, afraid to move because the marmot was so small.

"Yes," the marmot squeaked. "But I didn't expect you to be so big! I mistook you for a huge, dimpled stone and decided to get some sleep. Sorry!"

"Well, now you've found me! What are you going to do about it? Nobody will believe you," the dragon said thoughtfully.

"We marmots are very curious, you know?"

"How on earth do I know about marmots?" Fiery Wind chuckled.

The marmot was a little encouraged by such a friendly attitude and moved even closer to the dragon's head, which the dragon lowered to the ground to get a better look at the funny creature.

"Everyone calls me Zach," the marmot bravely introduced himself. "I don't care if other marmots believe me; I'm glad I was able to see a real living dragon for myself," he said and bowed slightly, as much as his tummy would allow him.

"Fiery Wind is my name," the dragon introduced himself, trying to breathe more quietly.

"It's better to climb on my head, closer to my ear, so it will be more convenient for us to talk and for me to breathe."

"With great pleasure," said the marmot, climbing onto the dragon's head, "thanks for the honour."

Zach was a polite animal and knew politeness often helps in some difficult situations. He also wanted to avoid the dragon's mouth with its massive teeth. He thought being on its head near its ear was much more comfortable and safer.

"Now you can tell me a few legends about myself," the dragon asked and listened. Zach scratched his head a little, getting comfortable and trying to remember a fairy tale that wouldn't offend his new friend.

Yes, the little marmot was already sure that they had become friends.

Zach sat on the head of the Fiery Wind Dragon and told him about knights, princesses, kings, and cities where people lived. About how marmots helped people, warning them of danger, and helped animals by alerting them with their whistles about the approach of hunters. The marmot talked about how cold winters are and how many exciting things happen if you stand and look without moving around. Life is everywhere, and where there is life, there are many stories.

The Dragon listened attentively, only screaming out at some point during the story that dragons do not eat and never have eaten princesses. On the contrary, princesses often asked for help before marriage if they did not like the groom. And, yes, in ancient times, people were much friendlier. Kings often invited dragons specifically to amuse and surprise the people.

Several days passed like this, the marmot only occasionally leaving the cave to look for food. And so, when Zach started to miss his family, he began to get ready to go home.

"I'm glad I got to know you," Fiery Wind told him.

"You are a brave and courageous marmot and quite smart. I liked you, and thank you for your fairy tales and stories. As a keepsake of our meeting, I will give you the five smallest scales from my tail. They will bring you good luck."

With these words, the Fiery Wind flicked its tail, and five beautiful dragon scales with a sharp protrusion in the middle fell in front of Zach. They shimmered in the sun's rays with all the colours of the rainbow. Zach was thrilled with the gift!

"Now they will believe me that dragons exist; thank you, Fiery Wind! I have a dragon friend!" The marmot even danced on the spot with pleasure and praise.

Fiery Wind laughed and offered to give his new friend a ride home. Little Zach's happiness knew no bounds! After all, almost everyone in his family laughed at his idea of going on a journey to find a living dragon. Nobody believed that he would succeed. Everybody scared him that there were many dangers on the road. And if he meets a dragon, he will undoubtedly be eaten.

And so, little Zach returns to his valley on a real dragon. Yes, that's how it was!

Many years later, a traveller found these five dragon scales in a beautiful meadow and was amazed at their beauty, shape, and patterns.

He decided to build a house and make tiles on the roof shaped like dragon scales because he had already guessed who they belonged to.

The tiles may not shimmer so brightly in the light of the sun's rays, but they will always remind people that giant dragons still live somewhere in deep caves.

25

Three Dragons

This incredible story took place in ancient times when dragons lived amongst people.

You might know that dragons are noble, majestic, and wise creatures. They do not live in a pack but prefer solitude and are happy doing so. Don't believe that dragons are bloodthirsty and eat princesses.

This is wrong. Dragons are ancient mythical creatures, and they receive their energy for life from the four elements: Earth, Air, Fire, and Water. Dragons love to fly and are very curious, but whether a dragon will become your friend depends only on you. Who knows, maybe you will meet a dragon someday. If you do, then remember this story.

In this particular land, there lived three dragons. They were different in colour and also very different in character.

The first dragon was covered in reddish-purple scales. It loved to breathe fire, considered itself omnipotent, and never listened to advice from others. Nor was it interested in the opinions of other dragons, even less those of people. In those days, people had to ask dragons for assistance, but persuading this dragon to help was difficult.

The second dragon was covered in blue-green scales. It loved to swim in the sea and big rivers and always listened carefully to everything it was told but always made its own mind up in the end.

This dragon was easy to get along with and willingly helped people and other creatures rather than simply for amusement.

The third dragon was covered in gold-orange scales and was called a sun dragon for that reason. It was utterly useless to ask this dragon for help. This dragon believed it was above all this fuss, loved to fly in the clouds, closer to the sun, and returned to its cave only to rest. It can sometimes be seen in the night sky, but people have stopped believing in dragons and believe that they are all comets.

Although these three dragons were different, they were united by many things.

They all valued kindness, courage, beauty, and harmony. So, the golden dragon could spend hours admiring how the sun's glare plays on the sea waves or how the light plays on the faces of a diamond.

A young fisherman lived in a village near a river. From early morning, he fished on the river bank, then went to the city or the nearest town and sold his catch there. That's how he lived. He was young, happy, handsome, and, as it seemed to him, lucky. He almost did not wish for a better life for himself. But everyone has their destiny, and sometimes this brings surprises.

Fishing in the early morning, when the sun was just emerging from the horizon, from afar, he watched a Blue Dragon bathe in the river, and the Sun Dragon fly above the clouds. It was always an extraordinary sight. The fisherman believed that luck had smiled on him and that the whole day would be wonderful.

The fisherman lived alone in a small wooden house, which he inherited from his grandfather, whom he loved very much and who was a great teacher to him. But our fisherman knew nothing except fishing, the river, and his village. He only visited the city occasionally and then only for the market to sell his fish and buy groceries.

He was always in a hurry to return home as soon as possible.

On one of these typical days, a town crier came to the village and announced the king's decree. The decree stated that the king was looking for a daredevil brave enough to bring him magic scales from the chest of each of the three local dragons. For this, the king promised to take the hero to the palace, make him his nobleman, and pay a good reward.

Every resident of the city or village understood that the task was practically impossible, and everyone was too busy with their own lives. Who knows what will happen in the king's palace? Kings are always very capricious, and you should not trust them.

Our young fisherman also heard the king's decree but did not even imagine how this task could be done. Nobody actually knew where the dragons lived. Even finding them would be incredibly difficult.

Our young fisherman had no desire to become a hero or noble in the palace, and the king's decree saddened him. The young fisherman understood that one could only get dragon scales by killing them, and he didn't want that. He liked dragons, their strength and majesty, how they soared in the sky. He was always glad that they lived somewhere nearby, like a miracle.

Each day that passed, the young fisherman

looked anxiously towards the mountains, but the dragons did not appear. The people in the village began to say that brave souls had been found, and they were going on a campaign hunting down the three dragons to get their magical scales. The young fisherman did not understand how it was possible to kill such beautiful creatures for the sake of scales, even if they were magic. He became despondent, so much so that one day, he decided to find the dragons himself and warn them of the danger, no matter the cost. He collected food, filled a flask with water, bought himself more robust shoes for climbing the mountains, a warm sheep's wool cape if it was cold, and set off for the mountains early in the morning.

On the first day of the journey, he did not meet anyone, and there was no one to ask. He remembered the direction where the blue and gold dragons flew and decided that he would go towards that direction.

So, he walked and walked, crossed stormy mountain rivers, met mountain goats who looked at him in surprise, climbed higher and higher into the mountains, and spent the night in small caves and just under trees, but he did not come across any dragons.

Of course, the shepherds who graze the sheep saw dragons high in the sky, but they didn't know where they lived.

Days passed, and the young fisherman lost hope of finding the dragons but decided to climb one last peak. If he did not find them, he would return home.

And just that night, a strong thunderstorm broke out. The wind moved huge boulders from their place, so they rolled down far from where they were. This storm soaked the young fisherman through and through; he was frozen and had already decided to return home as soon as the storm subsided. So, in the dark, through the wind, he made his way along steep mountain slopes in search of a cave or at least some hollow in the mountain to shelter from the wind and rain.

Soon, he saw a tall tunnel going deep into the mountain. Lightning illuminated the way for the young fisherman, and he made his way deeper in search of a dry and quieter place as he was exhausted. Suddenly, he saw a fire a little further inside. The young fisherman was very happy. Finally, he would be able to warm up, and quite possibly, someone would feed him.

He walked no more than another twenty meters inside when he stopped in surprise. It really was a small fire in a hearth of stones that fit tightly together. He had never seen anything like this before. Warmth came from the stones, and the young fisherman decided to lie down and rest a little.

He didn't notice anyone around and decided to wait for the owner and thank him. Sleep quickly overcame the fisherman.

During that night, the young fisherman has a fantastic dream that he visits a blue dragon. The colossal creature, bowing his head, looks attentively at him. The young fisherman jumps up and, at first, is scared but soon pulls himself together and silently stands before the dragon, looking straight into its eyes.

"So," the dragon grins, "Guests came to me. Tell us why you are here."

The young fisherman decided to tell everything straight, as it is. He was a simple man and did not like to lie or pretend. He explained to the blue dragon about the decree, the king's request for dragon scales, and the brave souls who would soon look for all three dragons.

"And why should I believe you?" the dragon grinned again. "You're sleeping now. I decided to talk to you only because you found my cave. You are my guest. Still, thank you for deciding to talk about this. People can find us only if we allow it ourselves."

"But I saw you swimming in the river several times while fishing early in the morning. So, you are coming to our world, too."

"Hmm... noticed... so you saw me? I don't like people with their fuss and desire to catch everything that moves, like your fish, for instance."

"I catch fish for food for myself and others; it helps me live." the young fisherman was offended.

"This is understandable, but not everyone is like you. Your king, for example, needed our scales but didn't say why he needed them. And I will say that for your world, dragon scales are like a cure for all diseases; they attract wealth, or you can find other uses for them. That's why your king decided to become richer and stronger. He didn't go to ask himself but sent brave men who are not heroes at all, as they think.

They have no idea how to kill a dragon. Only another dragon can kill a dragon, and no one else. And they need to learn politeness," the dragon grumbled. "How old are you?"

"22 years have passed since I was born."

"And I'll soon be 873." The blue dragon raised his eyes to the ceiling of the cave. "Okay, this is all talk. As you already understand, the royal daredevils will not be able to kill us, but they will disturb our peace. I need to fly down and talk to the other two dragons. Do you want to fly with me?"

The young fisherman almost woke up in surprise! Of course, he really wants to fly on a dragon. He was dreaming, and everything was as if it were real.

"Thanks a lot!" the young fisherman thanked the dragon and hesitantly approached him.

"Climb up the notches on the scales," the dragon instructed.

The young fisherman did so, and they, leaving the cave, soared into the sky and flew. They flew quickly, and the wind blew across the young fisherman, just like in the real world and not in a dream; the spikes on his neck and head were rough, and the young fisherman tried to be careful to avoid getting hurt. Soon, they began to descend. A rock ledge on a cliff hid the entrance to a vast cave. There was snow all around, and it was cold.

The Blue Dragon made a strange sound in its throat, and the young fisherman heard an answer that sounded like it came from the deepest depths of the mountain. Instead of a cave in the mountain, it was another large tunnel, into which he and the dragon began to enter. The red-crimson dragon was waiting for them, holding its head high. And when the blue dragon landed, he asked with a frown:

"I don't recognise you, my friend; what kind of stranger did you bring me on your shoulders? Why was he given such an honour? This is a simple man from the breed of people."

"Greetings! Funny stories are happening in the world of people; they are back to their old ways and trying to find us.

I brought you this young fisherman so that you can hear from him for yourself what the king is planning against us and whether we should help him next time. People are getting annoying."

The young fisherman again had to repeat everything. The red dragon listened attentively and even spat out flames twice when he laughed at the king's decree.

"It would have been easier to ask. After all, the king knows how to find us. He Just needed to ask in his dream about meeting; it couldn't be easier! Or is this a new young king, and this knowledge was not passed on to him?"

While the dragons were talking, the young fisherman looked around the unique tunnel.

All its walls, every centimetre, were painted with mysterious signs and drawings of other creatures he did not recognise. It looked so beautiful, so bizarre. Many questions arose in the young fisherman's mind, but he dared not ask or bother the dragons.

"Enough talk," the Red Dragon suddenly said, "let's fly to the Golden One, let's visit our mutual friend."

The young fisherman again climbed onto the shoulders of the Blue Dragon, and they rose from the tunnel up to the sky. And again, they flew for a long time, and the young fisherman looked at the valleys with tiny villages below; this is how they looked from above. The rivers reflected the sky's blue colour.

They curled like ribbons, narrowing and branching. Everything was beautiful from above: the forest, the fields, and the sea in the distance.

Soon, they landed on a high hill covered with thorny bushes. At the top of the hill stood an overgrown pyramid, which was difficult to distinguish from being part of the hill since it was all covered with moss and lichen. But if you look closely, you can see that this hill had four sides for some reason. The golden dragon lay at the foot of the pyramid, sadly resting its head on its paws, and looked at a beautiful flower in front of its nose.

Neither dragon was in a hurry to disturb it; everyone settled around and silently watched the Golden Dragon. The young fisherman could not stand it and asked quietly in the Blue Dragon's ear why everyone was silent.

"But we are not silent," the Golden Dragon suddenly said and stood up, "We talk like that. We can talk silently; can you people also do this?" looking carefully at the young fisherman.

"We can't," was all he could say.

"I already know your news, which is no longer news. It's unclear why your king suddenly wanted to fight with us. We all like these places so much, and now we must leave them and look for calmer ones."

"Nooo!" The young fisherman cried out, "Don't fly away! Our world would become completely different without you! We all, everyone, need something extraordinary in life. Take me for example. Early in the morning, I was in a hurry not only to catch fish, but I had always hoped to see a blue dragon swimming in the river! What could be more beautiful than this? This incredible sight lifted my soul to heaven and made me stronger and happier. I think other people feel this, too! What do I care about the stupid king who decided to compete with you in strength? He is probably weak and unsure of himself.

To know that a dragon, or even three, live nearby is incredibly lucky, it's like feeling protected, it's like knowing that there are many secrets and mysteries in the world that people will have to solve for many centuries," the young fisherman said passionately and began to cry. He understood he could not change the dragons' decision to fly away.

"Look how eloquent he is," the Red Dragon smiled, and the Blue Dragon nodded, causing the young fisherman to fall head over heels and find himself in the middle of a triangle of three dragons. Which made all three dragons laugh together.

"Fate sent us a good sign with you, fisherman. It would seem the time has come for us to leave your World," the Golden Dragon concluded.

"You are a brave, courageous, intelligent, and kind person; we will take you back home and make three circles over your village so that every person there can see us and believe that there are dragons in the world. Each of us will also give you one of our scales as a keepsake from us. Use them wisely. Our third gift is that we will allow you to talk to one of us and ask for advice. You already know how to do it. Until now, this has always been a gift to the king in power. But since his attitude towards us has changed, we are giving this gift to you for the rest of your life."

After these words, the Golden Dragon picked a beautiful flower and, holding it in its mouth, soared into the sky. And behind it is the Blue Dragon with a young fisherman and the Red Crimson Dragon. They, as promised, made three circles over the village of the young fisherman, and he woke up at home in his bed, raised in surprise on his arms, and looked around. The room shimmered with all the rainbow colours as three large scales lay on the table: red-purple, blue-green and gold with orange tints. And they shone so brightly that people who passed by began to look into the windows of his house, amazed at this radiance.

What happened next is another story.

Mira
and her
Dreams

Mira sat by the window and dreamt.

In her opinion, her dreams were different and always unique.

She knew that if you dream of something good, it will come true.

So, whenever the girl got what she wanted, she felt like a fairy or a princess.

Mira also loved dragons very much, different ones; it didn't matter which ones, she loved them all: dragons in books, cartoons, toy dragons, and real ones. Yes, Mira knew that dragons only live in fairy tales and are wise creatures that can fly.

One of the girl's most cherished desires was to meet a real dragon and, if lucky, fly on it.

Why not? Mira was sure that somewhere, there was a world in which dragons lived.

She already had several toy dragons and two books on the subject.

And now, her favourite white dragon sat in front of the girl and looked at her slyly with one eye.

The autumn rain was drizzling outside, and she sat on the windowsill and continued her daydream. Thoughts flowed in her mind like a quiet river, and then, suddenly, the girl recalled her special collection, a box of good memories. Mira remembered it and smiled - it always lifts the mood if you think about something pleasant.

The box contained two beautiful cones from the forest, a shell that lets you hear the sea, a ribbon from a New Year's gift, a bracelet made of bright ropes, which she exchanged with a friend for a beautiful transparent pebble, a multi-coloured magic pencil and several other interesting items.

And then, outside the window, something incomprehensible appeared in a flash. Mira opened her eyes wide, trying to understand what it was and whether she should be scared and call her mother.

But nothing special happened anymore, and Mira dozed off again, hugging her friend, the white dragon.

She dreamed that she was standing on the edge of a cliff, in a beautiful valley between two rocks, and watching dragons fly about.

Mira looked around; everything looked like it was in real life, but the dress she wore was long and fluffy, and a small tiara was on her head. In her arms lay her beloved white dragon, only now he was alive and heavy. The little dragon jumped to the ground and said:

"You wanted to talk to the dragon, my princess; I have brought you to a world where dragons live. Now my friend will arrive, and you can talk to him. Just remember that now, in this world, you are a real princess."

Mira couldn't believe this was happening to her. She even sat down on the grass and silently watched the mesmerising flight of dragons in the distance. The white dragon immediately jumped into her lap and rubbed its head against Mira's hand.

"You dreamt, and I helped you, but all this will not last long. Soon, you will return to your world, home to your mum and dad. Don't be sad!"

But Mira was not sad; this magical place enchanted her.

Purple mountains, translucent from the fog, rose to the left and right and were covered with multi-coloured forests.

Below, in the valley, the river sparkled in the sun, birdsong could be heard everywhere, and the breeze gently played with flowers and grass. Dragons flew, soared, and played with each other high in the sky among the clouds.

Yes, these were real dragons, exactly how Mira imagined them.

"It's so nice and beautiful here," the girl finally said, stroking the white dragon.

"Yes, I love being here too! Look, look, my friend is flying towards us. Be careful; he is very big and a little clumsy," the little dragon jumped for joy and exhaled a stream of flame towards the sky.

Mira didn't have time to look back when a huge shadow covered her, and she was overcome with heat. Although she was brave, she closed her eyes in surprise and covered her face with her hands. When she reopened them, she didn't immediately understand what she saw.

In front of her, on the grass, two huge, clawed paws covered with scales towered above her. Mira slowly raised her head up and up again. To her surprise, she fell on her back and laughed. She could now see an enormous dragon of inexpressible beauty, shimmering in blue and green colours in the sun.

"Hello, Princess Mira," said the Dragon, bowing his head in front of the girl.

Mira jumped up, brushed off her dress, and took a few steps back... Suddenly, she swayed and began to fall from the cliff. All this took only a second or two; Mira didn't even have time to get scared before she found herself on the back of her new friend. The dragon had caught the girl and soared into the sky.

"My princess, excuse me and let me introduce myself," Mira heard a low, rumbling voice, "my name is Clog, and I'm glad to see you in our world," the dragon turned his head to her. His back was broad, with many spikes, which the girl held on to, sitting comfortably between them.

"Hold on tight; we will fly a little over this valley, my princess!"

Mira smiled and remembered her friend, the little white dragon.

"Your friend is waiting for you over there on a rock; don't worry," Clog rumbled as if he had read her thoughts.

Mira looked down and around at other surprised dragons and birds flying past, at the colourful trees on the cliffs, at the castles and houses far below beside a river...

Everything was much better and clearer than in her dreams. Mira laughed happily when Clog made a sharp turn, soared up, and then dived down; the girl was not afraid.

Finally, the dragon flew up to the rock with the white dragon and landed a little further from the edge.

Mira carefully climbed off Clog's back and stood in front of him.

"Thank you, Clog; I am very grateful to you for this journey! This was my dream, and it came true!"

"My respect, Princess Mira! I am very pleased with our meeting, and I ask you to be my friend! At any moment in your life, when you feel sad, remember me, the dragon named Clog, and I will try to help you! But one way or another, if you believe in the best and know how to dream, everything in your life will always be good. Trust the dragon!"

After hesitating, she asked if he could give her something to add to her collection of good memories.

"Of course, I'm glad to do this for you! When you return home, you will find my gift!" said Clog and, moving back a little, soared into the sky, swaying its wings as it flew.

The white dragon jumped into Mira's arms, and she opened her eyes... at home.

It was still raining outside the window, and the white dragon was lying on the girl's lap. Next to her, on the windowsill, she saw a flower. It was a flower from the world where dragons live. The girl put it between the pages of the book to keep forever.

And now, when she has become an adult, she picks up this book from time to time, and the book immediately opens on the page with the gift. Mira smiles and makes a wish!

Thank you!

Thank you for reading our kind stories.

There is some truth in every fairytale!

Be brave, read more interesting stories and fairytales and magical doors to other adventures will start opening for you.

Special thanks

Special thanks to Igor Kirko and Zinaida Kirko for the practical advice and support in creating the book and illustrations.

My thanks also to Leslie Harwood, an excellent translator and kind editor.

Published books of
our project:

The Happy
Story
Garden

WHO WILL I BE WHEN I GROW UP

THREE SHORT STORIES ABOUT KINDNESS

THREE SHORT ADVENTURE STORIES

THREE STORIES ABOUT FRIENDSHIP

THREE STORIES ABOUT FAIRIES

THREE STORIES ABOUT ANIMALS

THREE STORIES ABOUT DRAGONS

The pocket Oracle

Victoria Harwood

THREE INCREDIBLE ADVENTURE STORIES

BLAME THE MONSTER!

Victoria Harwood

WELCOME TO
THE HAPPY STORY GARDEN

https://thehappystorygarden.co.uk

Milton Keynes UK
Ingram Content Group UK Ltd.
UKHW050629010424
440413UK00005B/25